DATE DUE

d/95

First published in the United States in 1994 by
The Overlook Press
Lewis Hollow Road
Woodstock, New York 12498

Library of Congress Cataloging-in-Publication Data

Ross, Tony.
Hansel & Gretel / Tony Ross.
p. cm.
Summary: a retelling of the well-known tale in which two children
are left in the woods but find their way home despite an encounter
with a wicked witch.
[1. Fairy tales.   2. Folklore—Germany.]
I. Hansel and Gretel.
English.   II. Title.
PZ8.R668Han 1994
398.21—dc20
[E]
93-31047
CIP
AC
ISBN: 0-87951-535-X
135798642

Printed in Italy

·Hansel and Gretel·

Tony Ross

The Overlook Press
Woodstock · New York

A very long time ago, a woodman lived with his two children in a dreary shack in a dreary wood. The boy was called Hansel, and his sister, Gretel.

The woodman's good wife had died years ago, and when he married again, his new wife was jealous of the two children.

When times were hard and food was scarce for the table, the new wife found a way to rid herself of Hansel and Gretel.

"Take 'em away and dump 'em in the forest," she told her husband.

"No!" he said. "I love them."

"They are two extra, useless, sniveling mouths to feed," she snarled.

"I love them," said the woodman.

"You ought to love me more," said his wife, over and over again.

"Oh, dear!" sighed the woodman.

Now Hansel overheard the plans to dump himself and his sister in the forest, so, one night, he slipped out and filled his pockets with white pebbles.

The following day, the woodman took the children off to work with him. "Goodbye, darlings," called the stepmother, as the three set off for the deepest forest.

Hansel trailed along behind the other two, and every few feet he dropped a white pebble onto the ground.

The woodman sang songs to Gretel, but his heart sobbed at the thought of leaving the children in the wild forest.

As evening approached, the woodman told his children to sit down and rest. Then, with a sad backward glance, he slipped away.

As it grew darker, Gretel began to worry. "Where's Dad?" she moaned. Of course, Hansel knew exactly where Dad was: he was on his way home by himself.

The sun went, and the moon came.

"I wish Dad would come," wailed Gretel. "I think this place is creepy."

"Better not let her know Dad's gone off and left us," thought Hansel. Then he said, "Come on then, we'd better go. We'll see Dad at home."

"We're lost!" wailed Gretel.

"No we're not," said Hansel. "All we have to do is follow this trail of pebbles. They'll take us right back to our own front door."

The small white stones gleamed like cat's-eyes in the dark, and by morning, the children were home again, just in time for breakfast.

The woodman was overjoyed. "Sweetie-pies!" he shouted.

"Pooh!" spat the stepmother.

The stepmother ranted and raved all day, and finally, the woodman set off back into the forest, to try and lose the children again.

This time Hansel had no time to gather pebbles, so he dropped small pieces of bread to mark the way.

Afternoon turned into evening, and the two children were so tired that they tumbled into a sleepy heap beneath a bush. The woodman kissed them both, and crept sadly away.

As they slept, birds of every kind swooped out of the trees, and gobbled up the path of bread for their supper.

An owl was just making off with the last piece of bread, when Gretel woke up.

"Hey!" she cried. "That's ours. How can we find our way home now you've eaten our path?"

The owl put the bread down and blinked at her. "Come on!" he said. "That little scrap's no use to you. Let me have it, and I'll show you the way home."

So the children followed the owl, who was not as good as his word.

He took them to the strangest house, built of cake, with an icing roof, and a garden fence of gingerbread men.

Hansel and Gretel knocked on the door, then started back, as a nose popped out of the mailbox.

It was not a nice nose, and it was green. The nose sniffed for a moment, then the door opened.

An old woman lived in the house, and she seemed nice enough, for after hearing the children's story she sat them down at the table.

"You must have some supper, dearies," she giggled, "and then you must stay the night, in a soft bed with clean sheets, and tomorrow I will put you on the path to your home."

But there was something wrong . . .

. . . There were tadpoles in the jelly.

After supper, the children went to bed. The bed *was* soft, and the sheets clean, and soon they fell asleep.

Around midnight, in crept the old woman with the green nose. Gently, she lifted Hansel, and quickly she took him away.

Along almond corridors, and down marzipan stairs they went, then down some stairs that turned to stone. Suddenly, Hansel woke up. He was about to scream, when the old woman threw him into a cold cellar, knocking the breath from his body. The door slammed shut, and the lock went clunk.

The old woman didn't pretend to be nice any more. She told Hansel she was going to fatten him up for her dinner, so he'd better get used to the idea.

Every day she brought him *huge* meals, and every day she said the same thing.

"Put your finger through the bars, dearie, and let me feel how plump you're getting."

And every day Hansel pushed a chicken bone through, and every day the old woman pinched it.

"Why, dearie," she snarled, "I do declare you're getting thinner, I can't eat you today!"

All the time Hansel was getting huge meals, poor Gretel was hardly getting anything at all. What's more, she was having to do all the hard work. As she worked, she planned to free her brother.

At last her chance came. She had just lit a roaring fire in the stove.

"Oh dear," she cried, "this stupid fire *won't* light."

The old woman opened the door of the stove, and peered in.

"Silly goose," she cried. "The fire's . . ." but before she could finish, Gretel pushed her into the stove, and slammed the door.

The old woman roared, but not as loudly as the fire.

The stove roared, as if it were fired with magic coal, and the house began to shake. Gretel ran to the cellar and set Hansel free. As they climbed the cellar steps, the house began to crumble around their ears.

The stove was glowing red now, and leaping around the kitchen.

"You'll never get away from me!" it seemed to scream.

A chest fell from a high shelf, spilling precious stones, and jewelry. "Come *on*!" shouted Gretel.

"Hang on!" said Hansel. He was filling his pockets with precious stones. Gretel ran back, and took his hand.

"*Come on!*" she cried again, and the two of them dashed into the garden, just as the icing roof collapsed.

In the glow of the melting house, the gingerbread fence changed back into the children who were enchanted many years ago.

"Wow. . ." gasped Hansel. "Old Green Nose must have been a WITCH!"

"Have you only just figured that out?" panted Gretel, as everybody scattered into the cool forest.

When Hansel and Gretel stopped running, they found themselves on the banks of a wide river. A swan drifted lazily by on the current.

"Oh dear," sighed Gretel. "How on earth are we going to cross that?"

"No problem," said the swan, "I'll take you across."

"You are kind," sighed Gretel.

"Not at all," said the swan. "Business is business! The fare is … everything you have in your pockets."

Hansel groaned, but there was nothing else to do. He emptied his pockets, and handed over the jewels and precious stones.

With murmured thanks, the swan carried the children over the river, and soon they found their way home.

The woodman greeted his children with tears of joy.

"Funny thing 'appened!" he laughed when they had finished hugging. "This morning a terrible roar 'appened in the forest. There was a great ball of fire, a smell of burnt cake, and my wife just vanished."

Then Hansel and Gretel told him all about their adventures.

"The sad thing is," said Hansel, "we had to give all the jewels away."

"All except *this*," said Gretel. Underneath her cap, she had hidden a giant pearl, enough to keep the three of them in comfort for ever after.

"The swan only asked for everything in our *pockets*!"